We Go in a Circle

Peggy Perry Anderson

Houghton Mifflin Company Boston 2004

Walter Lorraine Books

To all the servants of the All Star Therapy Ranch.

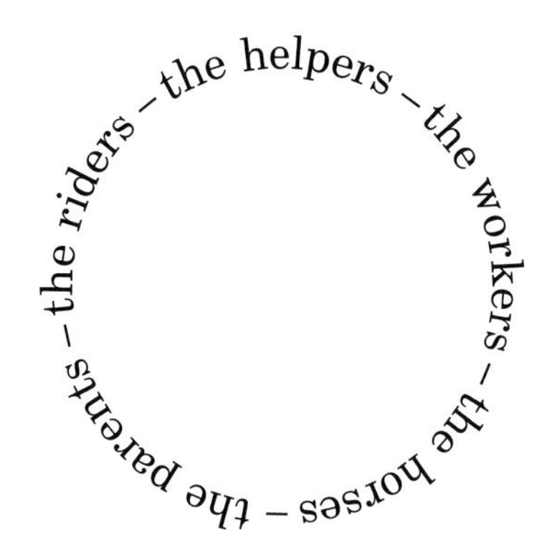

A special thanks to ranch owners
Bob and Alice

Walter Lorraine Books

www.houghtonmifflinbooks.com

Library of Congress Cataloging-in-Publication Data
Anderson, Peggy Perry.
We go in a circle / by Peggy Perry Anderson.
p. cm.
"Walter Lorraine books."
Summary: An injured racehorse is rehabilitated to carry riders in hippo therapy—
horseback riding used as physical therapy.
ISBN 0-618-44756-3 (hardcover)
1. Race horses—Juvenile fiction. [1. Race horses—Fiction.
2. Horses—Fiction. 3. Horsemanship for people with disabilities—Fiction.] I. Title.
PZ10.3.A4945We 2004
[E]—dc22
2004000567
ISBN–13: 978-0-618-44756-5

Printed in Singapore.
TWP 10 9 8 7 6 5 4 3 2 1

I am a racehorse.

We go in a circle.

The strongest and the fastest wins.

When I win, I feel special.
I feel important.

But one day
I hurt my leg.

I couldn't race anymore.

When horses can't race anymore,
they are taken away and we
never see them again.
That's just the way it is around here.

It was true. Someone came
and took me away.

But the new place had a barn.
And there were other horses
in the pasture.

My new owner took care of me.
My leg got better.

One day helpers came. They combed me and brushed me. They made me feel special. They made me feel important.

They put a very unusual saddle on me.
Then I saw a boy in a chair. It had wheels.

They took the boy out of the chair
and put him on my back.

I made him feel special.
I made him feel important.

I give rides all the time now.

We go in a circle.

Some riders can’t walk. Some riders can’t talk.

Some riders can’t even see.

But when they ride,
they smile,

they wave,

and some of them even
play games.

Then helpers feel special.
They feel important.

We go in a circle. That's just the way it is around here.

Hippo therapy is the name for using horseback riding as physical therapy. It is used to help both adults and children. People with many different types of disabilities benefit from horseback riding. The rocking motion of the horse relaxes muscles that are too tight and strengthens muscles that are weak. Horseback riding also builds self-esteem, improves coordination and balance, and provides social interaction with other riders and volunteers.

The horses used for this type of riding are gentle, older horses who are trained to be at ease around a lot of people. Each rider has a helper walking on either side of the horse to make sure the rider is always balanced. Another volunteer leads the horse around the arena. Therapy ranches everywhere are always in need of volunteers. For more information on therapy riding or to find a ranch near you, search the Web Sites under "hippo therapy" or "horseback riding therapy."

"I love to ride. When I finish riding, my legs feel good and I can walk better. Bob is my friend forever!"

—Hunter, age twelve

(Hunter has been riding at Bob's ranch since he was eighteen months old.)